W9-BWJ-392

Beast Quest®

STING
THE
SCORPION MAN

BY ADAM BLADE

ORCHARD

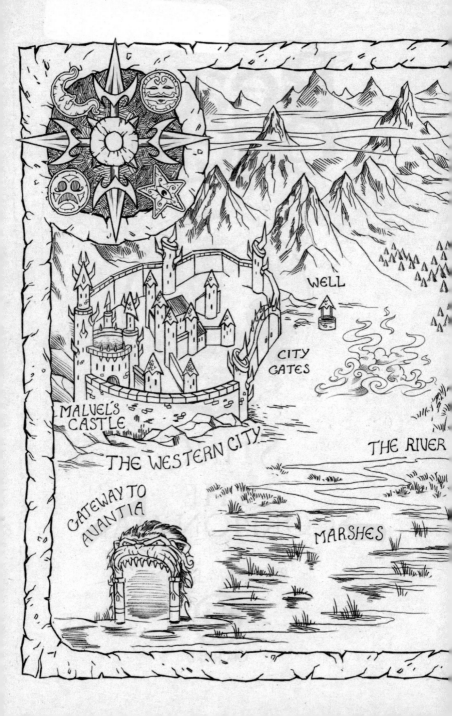

WELL

CITY
GATES

MALVEL'S
CASTLE

THE WESTERN CITY

THE RIVER

GATEWAY TO
AVANTIA

MARSHES

Gorgonia

REBEL SETTLEMENT OF KALOOM

DENSE FOREST

RAINFOREST

VALLEYS

THE BLACK OCEAN

RUINED CASTLE

CONTENTS

Welcome. You stand on the edge of darkness, at the gates of an awful land. This place is Gorgonia, the Dark Realm, where the sky is red, the water black and Malvel rules. Tom and Elenna – your hero and his companion – must travel here to complete the next Beast Quest.

Gorgonia is home to six of the deadliest Beasts imaginable – minotaur, winged stallion, sea monster, Gorgon hound, mighty mammoth and scorpion man. Nothing can prepare Tom and Elenna for what they are about to face. Their past victories mean nothing. Only strong hearts and determination will save them now.

Dare you follow Tom's path once more? I advise you to turn back. Heroes can be stubborn and adventures may beckon, but if you decide to stay with Tom, you must be brave and fearless. Anything less will mean certain doom.

Watch where you step...

Kerlo the Gatekeeper

PROLOGUE

The Gorgonian medicine woman twitched and muttered in her sleep. Her dreams were strange tonight.

A boy stood alone in a dark tunnel, his face bloody and streaked with sweat. In his hand was a battered wooden shield with six tokens embedded in its surface. Torches flickered along the long passageway, throwing the boy's shadow onto the wall, where it stood huge and alone.

The boy was suddenly dwarfed
by a second silhouette – a Beast
with a sweeping tail and monstrous
pincers which snipped and slashed
at the air.

A giant scorpion!

The medicine woman moaned
in her sleep as the silhouette grew

clearer. The creature was more than a scorpion. It was half-man!

The boy whirled around, raising his sword, as the Beast attacked with its razor-sharp pincers.

"Tom!"

A girl's voice screamed. It was Elenna, the girl the medicine woman had helped to heal. She stood with a wolf by her side and held a bow with an arrow in the bow-string. She let the arrow fly at the scorpion, but it bounced harmlessly off the creature's body. The boy stumbled and the Beast reared up, its pincers snapping viciously and slicing ever closer to the boy's head.

The medicine woman woke from

her dream with a gasp. She sat
upright, clutching her blankets, her
heart hammering. A tiny scorpion
lay at the bottom of her bed. She
got up, her eyes never leaving the
creature's glossy black body. Her
nightmare had saved her life. Many
Gorgonians had been found dead
in their beds because a poisonous
scorpion had found its way under
the covers.

She pushed her way out of the tent. The boy's face was still clear in her mind. Tom. She had heard that name recently. Elenna had mentioned it. Tom was her friend.

Shivering, the old woman tried to shake off the feeling of dread that had crept over her. The dream was a sign of things to come. She'd had premonitions before. She hoped this one was wrong.

"Stay safe, Elenna and Tom," she muttered, gazing up at the swirling red sky of Gorgonia.

Scorpions were bad enough.

A giant scorpion would be unstoppable.

1

DESTINY IN THE WEST

The blood-red light from the
Gorgonian sunrise peeped through
the trees as Tom and Elenna
made their way out of the forest,
their faithful companions, Storm
and Silver, ambling beside them.
Vulture-like birds croaked on the
branches overhead, and a thick
mist lay on the ground.

Tom led the way, holding Storm's bridle. He noticed that Elenna kept her hand protectively on one of Silver's shaggy shoulders. The wolf had been badly wounded two Quests previously, and had only just returned to Elenna's side. Tom and his friends had already freed five of Avantia's Beasts from Malvel's kingdom. Arcta the Mountain Giant was the last of the six Beasts being kept here against his will by the evil wizard. If they could free Arcta, their Quest would be complete.

Tom pulled his shield from his shoulder and studied the tokens set into its scarred wooden surface. Gifts from the Good Beasts, they usually glowed and vibrated when a Beast was in danger. But Arcta's eagle feather remained dark, and the shield had been still for far too long. Where was Malvel keeping the mountain giant?

"Still nothing?" Elenna asked.

Tom shook his head. "It's as if Arcta is somewhere so far away that the shield can't sense him." He pushed his shield over his shoulder again, refusing to meet Elenna's eyes. He didn't want to reveal his worst fear: that Arcta was already dead. "Perhaps the map will give us some clues," he said instead.

He took the smelly, worn parchment from Storm's saddlebag. Malvel had given them the map

when they first entered Gorgonia.
Each time they began searching
for a Good Beast the map would
give Tom a sign that he could use,
or a green line would snake across
its surface for Tom and Elenna to
follow. Usually these signs and
pathways would lead to trouble,
but it was the only map that Tom
and Elenna had.

"Nothing," Tom said,
looking down at the map in
disappointment.

"We can't trust it anyway," Elenna
pointed out as Tom put the map
away.

"You're right," Tom replied. "I'll
use my compass instead. It won't
let us down."

Tom's uncle had given him the gold compass on his first birthday as a hero. Instead of north, south, east and west, the words *Destiny* and *Danger* were inscribed upon

its face. The compass had belonged
to his father, Taladon, who was
once the Master of the Beasts for
Avantia and had disappeared when
Tom was a baby.

Tom held the compass and walked
in a complete circle. As he pointed
it to the west, the arrow whirled
several times and came to rest on
Destiny.

Tom felt his heart lift. He put
the compass away. "The compass
is telling us to go west," he said
to Elenna. "I'm sure that's where
Arcta is. While there's blood in my
veins, I will find him and get him
home to Avantia!"

Storm neighed and tossed his
black mane as if he were agreeing.

Silver sprang ahead down the path, eager to get going, and Tom and Elenna pressed on after him.

In the far distance, they saw something lying on the ground.

"What's that?" Elenna asked, shading her eyes in the red light.

Tom used the power of the magical golden helmet to bring the object into focus. Although the precious Golden Armour had been returned to Avantia at the end of the last Quest, he still possessed its gifts, and the helmet gave him extra-keen vision.

It was a boy, sprawled on the ground and riddled with arrows. His body was twitching. Tom felt his skin turn cold.

"It's Seth," he said to Elenna.
"He's hurt."

Seth was one of Malvel's servants. Tom and Elenna had fought him before, and the boy had been intent on killing them.

"Do we help?" Elenna asked.

Tom hesitated.

Seth was his sworn enemy. What should he do?

1

DARK SURPRISE

Seth suddenly let out a groan of agony that echoed through the trees.

Tom knew what he had to do. He couldn't ignore another person in pain, even if that person was his enemy. To do such a thing would make him as bad as Malvel.

Tom tugged Storm's bridle, leading the black stallion towards the figure. Elenna walked next to him, with Silver pressed close to her side.

The path broadened and the trees thinned out to reveal a black, mirror-like lake. Seth lay close to the water's edge. He was still breathing, but only just. His ribcage rose and fell in shallow gasps. Six arrows were embedded in his chest, and his blood had seeped onto the ground. It seemed impossible that he was still alive.

Tom was now close enough to see the beads of sweat on Seth's forehead. Storm dug his hooves into the path then stepped backwards. His nostrils flared.

"Hush, Storm," Tom said, soothing his horse.

"Silver doesn't like this, either, Tom." Elenna gazed down at her wolf. Silver's growls were deepening, and the hair on his back was standing up.

"Seth can't do anything to us," Tom reasoned. "Look at him. He needs our help."

He gave Storm's bridle to Elenna.
Then he took hold of Epos the Flame
Bird's talon and pulled it from the
front of his shield, before kneeling
down next to Seth. As gently as
he could, he pulled three arrows
out of the boy's body and held the
phoenix's talon to each wound.
Seth's skin instantly began to knit
together, and one by one the wounds
started to heal.

Seth's groaning eased. His eyes
fluttered open. Seeing Tom, he cried
out in panic. "No! Leave me alone!"

Ignoring Seth, Tom pulled the
fourth arrow from the boy's chest
and healed the gaping hole.

Seth's eyes filled with terror. He
began pushing Tom away, as his

strength started to return. "You don't know what you're doing!" he gasped. "You should have left me to die!"

Tom ignored him. He took hold of the fifth arrow and pulled.

With surprising speed, Seth grabbed Tom's wrist and pushed the arrow back into himself with a scream of pain. Tom heard Elenna gasp with horror. Storm whinnied and tried to pull away from Elenna's grasp, while Silver stood still, his tail between his legs.

Tom could understand why his friends were so spooked. It was as if Seth wanted to die.

He steadied his hands and swiftly prised Seth's fingers away from the arrow, drawing the dripping shaft out of the boy's flesh.

"No," Seth moaned, as Tom took hold of the sixth and final arrow. "Don't do it."

"Something is wrong here, Tom," Elenna said, shaking her head. "I think we should respect Seth's wishes and leave him."

"He's mad with pain," Tom reassured his friend. "There's just one more arrow…"

Tom pulled the sixth arrow loose. Seth lashed out with his fists as Tom held the phoenix talon to the fifth and sixth wounds, but he was too weak to knock Tom's hands away. In an instant, the wounds had healed.

Seth let out an unearthly screech and writhed on the ground, making

Tom jump back in alarm. Elenna desperately attempted to soothe Storm and Silver as they tried to turn tail and run.

Something was happening to Seth. Something awful...

They watched in horror as the boy's legs fused together, forming a single limb that lengthened and tore through his clothes. It grew darker and harder until it turned into a bulbous, beaded tail. The tail swiped out powerfully at Tom and Elenna, knocking them both to the ground.

Seth screamed again. His voice sounded deeper and rougher. Three legs forced their way out of both sides of his torso, tearing through his tunic.

"Get back!" Tom shouted to Elenna
as they both scrambled to their feet.

Seth sprang onto his new legs
and let out a horrifying roar as his
arms stiffened and distorted into
two pincers. They began clicking

and snapping in Tom and Elenna's direction. Tom could hardly believe what was in front of him. The bottom part of Seth's body looked just like a scorpion, but his chest and head were still human. Seth pointed at Tom and Elenna, his face a mask of anger and despair.

"You!" he screamed, his voice terrifyingly deep. "This is your fault! This is Malvel's punishment for my failure. If you'd just let me die as I wished, this wouldn't have happened. I wouldn't be a monster!"

With a roar of fury, Seth picked up his sword, which had been lying by the side of the path. Its wickedly serrated edge glinted in the blood-red light. With his giant scorpion

pincers snapping, he advanced on
Tom and Elenna.

THE BATTLE
BY THE LAKE

"Don't come any closer," Tom ordered, pointing his blade at the creature in front of him.

Seth gave a ghastly chuckle. His long tail reared high in the air, ready to strike.

"Tom," Elenna gasped, staring up. "Look!"

Tom followed her gaze. Something

was gleaming at the tip of Seth's tail – a purple jewel. Instinctively, Tom touched the belt he wore around his waist – a belt already decorated with five jewels, each taken from the Beasts of Gorgonia... If Seth had a jewel, it could only mean one thing.

"Seth's an Evil Beast now," Tom whispered to Elenna. "The last one we must defeat."

"Enough talking!" Seth roared, lunging at them.

Elenna dived away, while Tom dodged to one side. He found himself next to the black lake that lay beside the path, and heard a rush of air as Elenna released her arrow. But the shaft bounced harmlessly off Seth's scaly tail.

Seth swung his sword above his head and sprang towards Tom. He moved so fast that Tom had to use the magical power of the golden boots to leap into the air and avoid the vicious blade. The tip of Seth's sword missed Tom's stomach by a whisker.

The momentum of Seth's attack carried him to the edge of the lake, where he teetered for a moment on the bank, desperately struggling to stay upright. Then he looked down at his reflection in the black water and Tom saw his face sag in horror.

"I'm hideous!" Seth screamed in despair, falling to the ground, away from his reflection.

Tom felt a surge of pity for the vile

creature in front of him, but there were no words that could possibly offer comfort. Tom turned and joined Elenna, who was standing with Storm and Silver. As he did so, a swirling red cloud dropped out of the sky and surrounded them. A tall wizard in dark green robes stepped out of the scarlet mist.

"Malvel!" Tom gasped.

The Dark Wizard inclined his head. "The young hero," he said, a thin smile spreading across his face. "I knew your good heart would get you into trouble one day."

Tom realised now that this was all part of Malvel's plan. The wizard had known he would try to help the injured Seth. Angrily, Tom levelled

his sword at him, ready to do
battle. But with a wave of one thin
hand, Malvel placed a shimmering
magical barrier in front of himself
and Seth. Growling furiously, Silver
hurled himself at the barrier, but

he bounced off the magical shield
with a yelp, almost as if he had been
burnt by fire.

"I beg you, Malvel," Seth sobbed,
collapsing before the wizard. "Turn
me back to how I was!"

Tom saw the wizard look coldly
at his servant. "Stop snivelling,"
Malvel commanded. "This is your

punishment for failing me so many times. You are no longer Seth, but shall be called Sting the Scorpion Man. And I command you, Beast, to go to the Western City of Gorgonia and guard Arcta the Mountain Giant."

Sting bowed his head in defeat.

Malvel conjured a shining red orb from the air, which pulsed and grew in his hand, then he threw it at Sting, imprisoning the new Beast in its blood-red heart.

Muttering in a language that Tom didn't understand, Malvel clapped his hands together three times. The giant red orb rose into the air and, with a flick of his long, bony finger, Malvel sent it west, towards the mountains. In an instant, the orb was out of sight.

The Western City. Tom gazed at the mountains on the horizon, committing them to his magical super-memory, a power he had won when he defeated Narga the Sea Monster. The orb may have flown too fast for him to follow its exact path, but Tom felt sure that the Western City lay somewhere in those mountains.

He was torn from his thoughts by Malvel's cruel and cackling laughter.

"I know what you are planning," sneered the evil wizard. "But don't bother to follow Sting. There is no way that you will ever find Arcta."

With a final screech of laughter,

Malvel wrapped himself in red mist and disappeared.

"He's wrong,"Tom told Elenna fiercely, pulling himself into Storm's saddle. "We will find Arcta and we will get him home."

Elenna nodded, looking as determined as Tom felt. Silver nosed around her feet as she picked up the arrow she had fired at Sting. She then slung her bow over her shoulder and climbed into the saddle.

Tom gazed to the west, where two Beasts – one good and one bad – awaited them. "We're coming, Arcta," he whispered. "And we will never stop looking for you. Not while there's blood in our veins."

4

THE VOICE IN THE WELL

The forest path wound along the shore of the black lake, emerging onto a wide open plain that ended at the line of black mountains where the red orb had disappeared.

Grabbing Malvel's map, Tom found the Western City. But the map was playing a new trick, one that Tom had never seen before. The image of the Western City floated across the ragged parchment, shifting mischievously from one place to the next.

"The map is no good to us," Tom said. "All we can do is head through the mountains and hope to find the Western City for ourselves."

Elenna nodded, and they pushed forwards.

Gradually the terrain grew rougher and the track narrowed as they approached the mountains. Tom rode Storm carefully, avoiding any sharp stones that might lame the stallion. Soon the path disappeared completely, and they had to weave through stunted black shrubs and trees, whose twigs and branches caught at their clothes and whipped cruelly across their skin. The blood-red sun climbed higher, and the air was searing hot.

After half a day of moving through the arid heat, they found themselves back on a stony path, and Tom spotted a cluster of dull red towers in a cleft between two mountains. He took out Malvel's map and looked at the image of the Western City, which flitted across the parchment like a ghost. Its walls were red, just like the towers he could see ahead.

"I think we've found the Western City," Tom said eagerly, reining in Storm so that the stallion could rest.

Elenna and Silver both sat down on the hot, dry ground. As Tom replaced the map in the saddlebag, he felt Storm's heaving sides. The stallion was panting heavily in the heat. Looking around, Tom saw a well a little further on.

He pointed it out to Elenna. "Let's get some water," he suggested, and guided Storm towards the well. Elenna and Silver followed close behind.

They leant over the circular wall of the well and peered inside, hoping to see a long dark shaft and the welcome glint of water at the bottom. But there was nothing but a pile of rubble and loose stones. The sides of the well had collapsed

inwards, blocking it up completely.
Tom rested his head on Storm's
sweaty flank. "I'm sorry, boy,"
he said. "We'll find some water

soon, I promise."

Storm whinnied trustingly and pushed at Tom's shoulder with his velvety black nose.

"Perhaps there will be another well closer to the city gates," Elenna said, shading her eyes from the glare of the sun as she stared up at the Western City. They were now a little closer, and the dark red walls gleamed in the sunlight.

"Hmm, I'm not sure that there are any more arou—"Tom broke off as the earth suddenly rumbled beneath their feet. Storm reared up, and Silver growled and retreated behind Elenna's legs.

"What was that?" Elenna said nervously. "An earthquake?"

Tom felt a tingling sensation rush up his arm from his shield. Arcta's token was vibrating! The earth rumbled again. The movement seemed to be coming from the broken well. Tom leant over the lip of the well and listened. The rumbling was an echoing roar. Tom recognised it immediately.

"It's Arcta!" he cried.

The giant roared again. The ground shook once more.

"What is he saying?" Elenna asked.

Thanks to the red jewel set into his belt, Tom could understand the Good Beasts of Avantia as never before. Now, he sensed the giant's rage. "He's angry," he said, trying to explain the feelings that were running through him as he listened to Arcta. "He's trapped somewhere underneath the Western City. He can't breathe properly – he feels like he's choking."

"We have to get underground straightaway and help him," Elenna said determinedly.

"Maybe we can climb down the well shaft and look for some kind of underground channel that will take us into the city," Tom suggested.

Elenna nodded. "You'll have to move some of these rocks," she said. "I'll help as much as I can."

The golden breastplate had given Tom the gift of great strength. He

seized the boulders that blocked
the mouth of the well and heaved
them aside as if they were feather
pillows. Elenna took care of some
of the smaller rocks. Before long,
they had cleared a dark space in
the well shaft. But the well's old
walls had relied for too long on

the support of the boulders, and now they collapsed. They could no longer hear Arcta's voice.

"It's no good," Tom said.

"We'll have to head into the Western City." Elenna said thoughtfully. "I'm sure we'll be able to find a way underground once we're there."

"True," Tom said. "If a giant the size of five men can be taken underground inside the Western City, then there'll be a very big trap door somewhere, right?"

"Right!" Elenna agreed.

Together, the four companions moved along the scrub-covered track that led to the gates of the Western City.

Tom hoped he was right about the trap door. They didn't have much time – and Arcta's life was hanging in the balance…

THE GATEKEEPER

As they approached the gates, Tom
felt all his senses sharpening. He
glanced around. From the moment he
and Elenna had arrived in Gorgonia,
Malvel had put a price on their
heads. Who knew how many bounty
hunters were waiting among the
rocks ready to capture or kill them?
The closer they got to the city, the
greater the danger became.

They won't catch us, Tom thought fiercely. *We'll fight to the death if we have to!*

The great red city loomed up in front of them. Its defensive walls towered overhead and were streaked with slime. Skulls were set into the brickwork and evil-looking spikes lined the top of the walls, their tips glinting in the red sun. The city's huge black gates were firmly closed. But there was no sign of any guards.

Silver growled uncertainly as Tom and Elenna stopped in front of the silent gates, and Storm pawed the ground anxiously.

Tom dismounted and gazed around. "Why are there no guards?" he asked Elenna.

"Perhaps it's a trap," Elenna replied uneasily.

There was a sudden movement from behind one of the trees that flanked the gates. A thin man in old brown robes, wearing a tattered eyepatch and holding a walking stick, stepped out to stand before them.

Tom recognised him at once.

"Kerlo!" he said.

"Hello," Kerlo replied. "If you wish it, I will let you into the city."

Tom wasn't sure that he trusted Kerlo, even though the Gorgonian gatekeeper had helped them more than once. Instinctively, his hand went to his sword. Elenna, too, held her bow and arrow at the ready.

Kerlo shook his head sadly. "Still so suspicious," he muttered. "Have I not been an ally on your Quest? Have I not aided you?"

"But why do you help us?" Tom challenged. "What's in it for you?"

Kerlo rested his weight on the long wooden stick that he held in his gnarled hands. "I was once a good wizard," he said quietly. "I tried to help the rebels in their fight against Malvel, but the Dark Wizard's magic was more powerful than I had ever imagined. He condemned me to spend an eternity as gatekeeper – between worlds." His face grew bleak. "I have not been able to cross a threshold in many years. I cannot even enter my family home." The gatekeeper fell silent for a moment. "You must understand, home is like a jewel and it is only once it has gone that you realise how precious it is."

"We thank you for all you have done, Kerlo," Elenna said. "Will you help us get into the Western City?"

Kerlo nodded. "Once inside, you must head to Malvel's castle," he said. "In the castle's courtyard, you

will find a trap door which leads to the cemetery that lies beneath the city. Those catacombs might be just the place to hide a giant Beast."

Kerlo held his hands out towards the gates. With a crash that shook the ground, the huge iron doors swung open. As they walked through them, Tom saw that the entrance to the city was set out as a series of three paths, just like the beginning of a maze. There were three possible routes into the city, but how could they be sure that they would choose the right one? And what would happen if they were wrong?

6

DANGER IN THE WESTERN CITY

Tom turned to ask Kerlo for advice. But the iron gates had already silently swung shut behind them and the gatekeeper was gone.

Tom thought quickly, then pulled out his silver compass. He aimed it at the path on their right. At once, the arrow swung to *Danger*. Tom moved the compass until it pointed at the central path. The needle flew to *Danger* again, quivering slightly this time. Then Tom turned the compass to the last of the three paths.

For what seemed an age, the needle hovered uncertainly. Tom was about to put the compass back into his pocket when the needle swung slowly around to *Destiny* and held steady.

"This way," said Tom, tugging at Storm's bridle.

They moved cautiously down the path. Blood-red walls flanked them on both sides. Overhead, the red sun hid behind black clouds, casting long, bruise-coloured shadows that seemed to bode ill.

An archway loomed up ahead. Two Gorgonian guards were patrolling it, their weapons slung casually over their shoulders. Beyond the guards, Tom and Elenna could see a city square surging with strange-looking people, whose bodies seemed to be hunched and crooked.

"I think we need to try the direct approach," Tom whispered.

Elenna nodded.

"Hail!" Tom called out, taking Storm with him as he strode towards the guards.

"Who goes there?" called the first guard in a harsh, croaking voice.

"Two travellers," Elenna replied, coming to stand at Tom's side. Silver bounded up next to her.

The second guard narrowed his eyes. His gaze flicked to Storm and Silver, then back again. "What is your business in the Western City?" he growled.

"Rest," Tom replied, holding firmly onto Storm's bridle. "Food. Will you let us pass?"

The first guard looked as if he were about to step aside. But then the second guard jabbed his finger in Elenna's direction. His eyes were suddenly full of greed. "I know you," he said. "You're wanted by Malvel. Your faces are on posters all over this city!"

The game was up. Using the power from his golden boots, Tom leapt and seized the guards around their thick necks, bringing their heads together with a loud *thunk*. The guards slumped to the ground, unconscious.

"Take their cloaks," Elenna said, looking all around her. "We can disguise our faces with the hoods."

Quickly they stripped off the guards' cloaks and flung them over themselves. After adjusting their hoods to make sure that no one could see their faces, they walked through the archway with Storm and Silver at their sides.

The city square was bustling with beings that didn't quite look human. Their eyes were yellow and their hair grew in ragged patches. Scarred, spotty skin hung loosely from their faces, and their teeth were black and pointed. With a shudder, Tom noticed that their hands looked like claws.

With their heads down, holding tightly onto Storm and Silver, Tom and Elenna walked across the square's glossy black flagstones.

Malvel's castle was impossible to miss. They could see it in the distance, on the fringes of the city. Forks of black lightning like huge lizard tongues flickered in the red sky above the castle's turrets, and Tom knew at once that it was the centre of all evil in Gorgonia.

The only way to reach the castle was to pass right through the centre of the city. Tom hoped that their disguises would hold out that long. He could see several "WANTED ALIVE" posters displaying their faces, stuck here and there on the city's slimy walls.

"There isn't much trade or bartering going on, is there?" Elenna whispered, glancing from

left to right as they hurried on. Tom
nodded. It looked as if the citizens of
the Western City were more inclined
to fight and argue than trade. Noisy
skirmishes were breaking out all
across the square.

A fight exploded between two men just as Tom and Elenna were passing.

"Give me my money!" screamed a ragged-looking fur-trader. "These are pure fox pelts!"

"Fox pelts?" his opponent roared back. "Cat pelts, more like. You won't get any money from me!"

There was suddenly a whirl of fists and kicking legs, which Tom and Elenna managed to sidestep. Silver was not so lucky. The wolf gave a high-pitched yelp of pain as the fur-trader's heavy-soled boot caught him in the ribs.

"Silver!" Elenna gasped.

Without thinking, she ran to her wolf's side and knelt down beside him. As she did so, her hood fell back, revealing her face.

There was a deathly hush in the square, followed by shouts of recognition. "Avantians!"

"Elenna!" Tom shouted, his own

hood falling away from his face.
"They know it's us! Run!"

MALVEL'S CASTLE

Hordes of Gorgonians lunged
towards Tom and Elenna, their
scaly arms outstretched and their
fists swinging. With his super-
strength, Tom threw off the
approaching attackers as easily as
if they were ragdolls.

Barrelling through the angry mob
he cleared a path across the square.
Elenna leapt nimbly onto Storm's

back, and the horse lashed out with his hard hooves as the Gorgonians tried to close in again. Elenna galloped after Tom, with Silver nipping fiercely at the ankles of any Gorgonian foolish enough to get in their way.

Tom grabbed his sword and flashed it left and right in warning. Elenna then galloped close enough for him to seize a handful of Storm's mane and pull himself into the saddle. They broke free of the attackers and raced towards the castle. Storm's black tail rippled out like silk, and Silver was a blur of grey fur as he sprinted at their side.

As they approached the castle,

Tom used his super-sight to check how many guards were on the gates. He didn't like what he saw. Two armed guards were on patrol. Various weapons hung from their waists, and they each held a wicked-looking sword.

Keeping out of sight of the guards, Elenna turned Storm's head and they raced into a copse of trees at the foot of the castle walls.

"We'll never get past them," Tom said, dismounting. "I'll send my shadow in to find an alternative route."

"Good idea," said Elenna, jumping from Storm's back.

The white jewel that Tom had won when he defeated Kaymon

the Gorgon Hound had given
him the gift of being able to send
his shadow away from himself.
However, Tom could not move while
he and his shadow were separated.
Tom and Elenna settled themselves
on a rock which gave a good view
of the castle.

"Go, shadow," he ordered. "Find a
way inside Malvel's castle."

The shadow peeled itself away
from him, slipping over rocks and
between trees, until it could press
itself up against the castle walls.
The guards noticed nothing. It
glided along the stone, feeling for
any nooks and possible entrances
with its thin black fingers.

"Anything?" Elenna whispered.

"Nothing yet," Tom said, standing absolutely still.

The guards' voices carried to where Tom's shadow was standing. Through his shadow's ears, Tom could hear that they were arguing.

"I'm leaving," one of the guards was saying. "You do what you want."

"But—"

"Our shift's over," said the first guard impatiently. "So what if the next guards haven't arrived?"

"We're supposed to wait till they get here..."

The first guard snorted. "Wait all you like. I've got better things to do."

Hardly able to believe his luck,

Tom watched through the eyes of his shadow as the first guard set off down the hill towards the city. After a moment's hesitation, the second guard followed. The gateway was clear.

Tom swiftly pulled his shadow back to him.

"Now's our chance," he told Elenna, jumping up into Storm's saddle. He held out his hand and helped his friend up behind him. "Quick, before the replacements get here."

Storm burst out from the cover of the trees and galloped through the unattended gate into the castle's courtyard, with Silver just behind.

Tom and Elenna leapt off the

stallion and gazed around in awe.
Malvel's castle was built entirely
from polished black stone, streaked
with gleaming stripes of red that
pulsed like veins.

The trap door Kerlo had
described was difficult to miss. It
was so big it took up more than
half of the courtyard.

"Just the right size for a giant,"
said Elenna grimly.

"Malvel must have taken Arcta
down here," said Tom, walking over
to where a huge iron ring was set
into the trap door. "There's no other
way he could have got him below
the ground."

Storm whinnied and Tom glanced
up at him. "We'll have to take

Storm and Silver with us," he decided. "It's too risky to leave them behind. The replacement guards will be here soon."

Kneeling down, Tom took the huge iron ring in his hands. He braced himself, and pulled.

Thanks to the great strength given to him by the golden breastplate, he was able to turn the ring easily and the trap door opened with a gentle creak. A gigantic hole was revealed beneath it. Damp stone steps led down into darkness.

Tom lifted the huge door to shoulder-height and rested for a moment. It was taking all of his strength just to hold it.

"I'm going to have to push the door right up and let it fall open," he said to Elenna. "Keep Storm and Silver out of the way."

"Won't that make too much noise?" Elenna asked, urging Storm and Silver to move back. "The guards will come running."

"We have no choice," Tom replied as he heaved the door upwards. "We've got to get down there and find Arcta."

He pushed the trap door all the way up, then let it fall backwards to the ground with a thundering crash.

Tom could hear shouts of alarm from deep inside the castle. "Follow the steps down!" he yelled to

Elenna, grabbing Storm's bridle. "The guards are coming!"

1

8

THE TOMBS

They raced down the steps into the yawning blackness of the tunnel. Tom yanked hard at the two long loops of rope that hung on the inner side of the trap door. Creaking and groaning, the door heaved slowly upwards and then came crashing down into place. Tom, Elenna and their companions crouched in the gloom and listened as guards ran into the courtyard above them. Their muffled voices drifted down through the trap door.

"What was that noise?" one said. "For a moment, I thought the master's castle was crashing down about our ears."

"Sounded like the trap door," grunted another.

Tom held his breath. What if the guards worked out that there were intruders underground?

A third guard scoffed. "The only way to open that door is with a team of men and some of the master's most powerful horses. It'll be the giant, no doubt, kicking and screaming below ground."

Tom felt Elenna tense beside him

at the mention of Arcta.

"He'll not be bothering us for much longer," said a fourth voice. "Come on – we need to find out what that noise was. Let's check the outer walls of the castle – maybe something has collapsed there."

Tom listened to the retreating footsteps as the guards left the courtyard.

"What did they mean about Arcta?" Elenna asked once everything was silent.

"I don't know, but time is running out," said Tom. "We need to move."

He looked around at the tunnel. There appeared to be only one path leading away from the trap door

and it was lit by flaming torches.
The walls were rough, and pools of
water lay in puddles on the ground.

Tom, Elenna and their animal
companions raced through the
twisting passageway, which sank
deeper into the ground with every
turn. The sides of the tunnel grew
smoother as they ran on, and Tom
noticed with a chill the tombs that
had been set into the tunnel walls.
He remembered Kerlo's words.
These were the catacombs: the
place where the Gorgonians of the
Western City buried their dead.

As he ran along, he couldn't help
but read the names on the tombs by
the flickering torchlight: *Memnon,
Arantis, Crestar, Xeropes...*

Taladon.

Tom stopped dead at the smooth black tomb bearing his father's name. His breath caught in his throat. Taladon wasn't dead. He was Malvel's prisoner. Wasn't he?

"Tom?" Elenna turned and came back up the tunnel to where he was staring at the black tomb. She held Storm's bridle tightly in one hand and Silver loped behind her, his eyes gleaming in the torchlight. "What's wrong?"

"I have to open this tomb, Elenna," Tom said fiercely, drawing his sword.

"There's no time, Tom," Elenna said. She seized his sleeve. "We have to save Arcta."

Tom shook off Elenna's hand. His father might be lying here, right in front of him! He took a step back and smashed the butt of his sword into the face of the tomb. The stone cracked. Tom slammed his sword into the tomb several more times until it buckled, revealing a gaping black hole. But there was nothing inside.

The tomb had never been used.

Elenna grabbed Tom's arm. "We have to hurry!"

Tom was about to reply when the red jewel on his belt began to glow and his head was suddenly filled with Arcta's voice. The mountain giant was telling him once more that he was finding it hard to breathe. Tom whirled round and stared down the tunnel. He suddenly understood. Arcta had been buried alive in one of these tombs!

Tom was filled with remorse. Why had he stopped to open Taladon's tomb? It had been a selfish thing to do and now Arcta's life was truly in danger. Tom knew that he would never forgive himself if they were too late!

"Arcta is in real trouble," he said to Elenna. "I've got to go."

"Hurry then; we'll catch up," Elenna replied.

Tom raced down the tunnel, using the speed given to him by the golden leg armour, and left his friends far behind. The walls blurred around him – and the tunnel suddenly opened up. Tom skidded to a halt. He was in an underground chamber with a low roof. A massive tomb like a great stone mountain stood in the centre of the room. A name had been carved in huge letters on the tomb's side.

Arcta.

Tom's head pounded. He could

sense that Arcta was weakening. There wasn't a moment to lose. He pulled his sword from its sheath and smashed it repeatedly into the side of the tomb. The echo of steel against stone boomed around the chamber. But the stone of this tomb was much thicker than that of Taladon's, and even with his huge strength, Tom couldn't break the tomb open.

Then he spotted a ledge, just above the tomb. If he could just get onto it, he could then try to lever the tomb open with his sword. Tom thought rapidly. The golden boots gave him the power to leap to great heights. He bunched his legs beneath him and jumped into the air, kicking off the giant tomb for an extra surge of height. With a thump, he landed on the stone ledge above the tomb. He then drew his sword and desperately started to lever up the lid.

Very slowly, it began to give. Tom worked hard, sweat pouring from his brow as he focused every drop of his magical strength on opening the tomb. At last, there was a gap wide enough for him to see into it.

Arcta lay very still, as if he were unconscious. His one great eye was closed. He was breathing in short, shallow gasps. Tom could see that he was bound by two huge silver chains that crossed over and around his vast, shaggy body.

With one more massive push, Tom shifted the lid off the tomb and stood on the side of the casket. He raised his sword above his head and brought it down on one of the chains that held Arcta. But the blade bounced harmlessly away, the impact sending fierce vibrations up Tom's arms. He tried again and again, but he soon realised that the chains were enchanted and would not break. Tom could feel despair threatening to overwhelm him. How was he going to free Arcta?

The sound of cantering hooves echoed down the tunnel, and Storm, Elenna and Silver raced into the chamber.

"I can't do it, Elenna!" Tom panted, shaking his head. "My sword isn't strong enough to break the chains!"

"Don't lose hope, Tom!" Elenna shouted up to him. "Remember the gift of the golden chainmail? Strength of heart! You must believe in yourself. You must believe that you can do it!"

Tom lifted his sword shakily above his head. Closing his eyes, he concentrated with all his might. He could feel the magic of the Golden Armour pulsing in him. Bringing the sword down with a yell, Tom cut clean through one of the chains, which slithered away from Arcta's body like a silver snake. The mountain giant's eye fluttered open.

"One more blow, and you'll be free," Tom promised, and raised his sword for the second time.

But before Tom could bring his blade down, a hideous, jet-black tail came crashing through the chamber's wall...

Sting!

9

TRAPPED!

Tom gripped his sword tightly, ready to fight, as the rest of the scorpion man's body smashed through the wall. How could he have forgotten? Malvel had sent Sting to guard Arcta. There was no way that he would let Tom free the mountain giant without a fight.

Fixing his gaze on Tom, Sting scuttled across the chamber

towards him. He raised his pincers and clashed them together, the ghastly sound echoing around the rough stone walls.

"At last," Sting said in a voice that no longer held any trace of the boy Seth. "I will have revenge for all that you have cost me."

Tom knew he had to find some extra strength to fight Malvel's last Beast. Everything depended on it.

He sprang from the edge of the tomb and tumbled through the air, landing squarely on Sting's back. With a roar, the Beast thrashed his tail, and the purple jewel at the end of it just missed Tom's eye.

With lightning speed, Sting spun around. Caught off balance, Tom fell to the ground. He pulled his shield from his back and flung it over his head as a giant pincer sliced towards him. The pincer bit into the edge of the sturdy wooden shield as if it were made of butter.

"Over here, Sting!" Elenna yelled, distracting the Beast as she drew back her bow and aimed an arrow.

"Leave us, girl," Sting said roughly. "This is not your battle."

"If your battle is with Tom then it's with me," Elenna retorted, releasing her arrow. It hit the Beast's stomach but his skin was like armour, and the arrow bounced off, falling to the ground. Sting roared in annoyance and turned to Elenna.

Tom staggered to his feet, eager to protect his friend, but Silver got there first, racing in to bite at Sting's scaly legs. Storm also cantered forwards and reared up, lashing out at the Beast with his hooves. Sting snapped his pincers like scissors, slicing at Storm's mane.

Tom felt a surge of pride as he saw his friends bravely fight the Beast. At the same moment, he heard a rattling sound from the tomb. Arcta was struggling against the second silver chain. His strength was returning! Tom gripped his sword tightly; he knew he needed to deal with Sting before he could free the Good Beast.

Tom called Storm and Silver away from the scorpion man, while Elenna let loose another arrow. This time it embedded itself in Sting's neck, which was still soft and human. With a screech of pain, Sting flung his hand to the arrow and tried to pull it out. It gave Tom the chance he had been looking for.

He raised his sword, and charged forwards, ready to strike at Sting's heart.

But Tom wasn't prepared for the Beast's powerful tail. It flew towards him like lightning. Tom just managed to avoid being crushed by its weight, but the jewel at the tail's tip cut deep into his cheek.

Tom could feel the warm blood trickling down his face. He looked up to see Sting's tail coming towards him again. With a surge of anger he whirled his sword and swung it upwards, slicing the tip of the tail clean off.

Sting screamed, the sound shaking the walls. The tip of his

tail flew across the chamber and hit the floor in a spurt of black blood. The purple gem came loose from its setting, rolling across the chamber floor towards Elenna. She bent down and snatched it up, sharing a triumphant glance with Tom. They had the final jewel!

Tom could hear Arcta still struggling to free himself from the second silver chain as Sting turned on Elenna, mad with pain. Tom tried to get past the Beast's injured tail, but even without its tip, it was still powerful and knocked him to his knees every time.

Suddenly there was a crash from the tomb. Tom whirled around.

"Arcta!" he shouted joyfully.

"You're free!"

The mountain giant had managed to pull himself away from the second chain. With a roof-shaking roar, he climbed to his feet and pounded on his chest.

The chamber walls trembled and fragments of rock cascaded from the ceiling as Arcta's head brushed the roof. The giant roared again, kicking away one side of his tomb, which fell to the floor with a mighty crash. The foundations of the chamber shuddered, and part of a wall crumbled into a heap. The movement of Arcta's huge bulk was putting a massive strain on the catacombs. The whole place looked and sounded as if it were about to crash down on top of them!

Sting backed away from Elenna
with a snarl, his eyes flickering
around the disintegrating chamber
before he turned and scuttled down
the tunnel towards the trap door.

Arcta bellowed loudly, raising

his arms. Tom could feel the Good Beast's wild delight at being free. More rocks began to fall to the ground.

"There's no time to lose," Tom called to Elenna. "We have to follow Sting, and get out of these tunnels before everything collapses!"

Narrowly avoiding a shard of rock that speared into the ground beside him, Tom grasped a handful of Storm's mane and pulled himself into the saddle. Elenna jumped up behind him. They began to gallop through the tunnel after Sting. Arcta lumbered after them, with Silver running alongside him.

Straining every muscle, Tom guided Storm between the crashing boulders that fell like giant black hailstones. Tombs smashed to the ground, spilling their bones into Storm's path. Grimly, Tom pushed on up the steep passageway. In the flickering light, he could see pools of sticky black scorpion blood on the ground. Tom knew that they had to catch Sting before he got to the trap door. He had no doubt that the Beast planned to leave them trapped in the collapsing chamber. Tom reminded himself that Sting had lost a lot of blood and would be getting weaker. There was still time to stop him.

The tunnel began levelling out, and ahead Tom could see Sting scuttling up the great stone steps towards the trap door. With what little strength he had left, the Beast heaved open the hatch and pulled himself out of the hole.

Tom leapt off Storm and sprang forwards.

But he was too late. With a resounding thud, the scorpion man slammed the trap door shut. The torches that lit the catacombs sputtered in the draught, and went out.

Arcta, Tom, Elenna, Storm and Silver were plunged into shaking, rumbling darkness.

PURPLE MIST

Overhead, Tom could hear Sting ordering guards to hammer Malvel's enchanted bolts into the trap door. The sound of banging started up immediately.

"I'm going to try to push the door open," Tom said, feeling his way up the stairs.

"Good luck," Elenna replied anxiously.

Tom tried with all his might to heave open the trap door. But even with the power of the golden breastplate, it would not budge.

Then Arcta gave a roar and lumbered up the stairs to help. Together, Tom and the mountain giant pushed at the trap door with all their strength.

"Be quick, Tom," Elenna said. "This chamber sounds as if it's going to collapse at any moment."

"It's no good," Tom panted, disappointment flooding through him. "Whatever enchantment Malvel has put on the bolts, it is too strong for Arcta and me."

Tom felt the giant's frustration rush over him like a wave.

"What are we going to do?" Elenna's voice trembled in the darkness. "There must be another way out."

The ground shook beneath their feet. The shuddering tunnel walls threatened to cave in at any moment. In that instant, Tom wished more than anything that he could be home in Avantia.

Kerlo's words suddenly echoed in his mind. *"Home is like a jewel,"* the gatekeeper had said. *"And it is only once it has gone that you realise how precious it is."* Had the gatekeeper been trying to give him some kind of clue?

"Do you still have Sting's jewel, Elenna?" Tom asked, leaving the stairs and feeling his way along the tunnel towards his friend.

There was a glow of purple light as Elenna drew the gem from her pocket. Tom took it carefully and held it up in front of him. The light began to pulse. Then Tom felt his hand begin to move through the air, drawing a doorway in the stone wall with the edge of the jewel. With a rush of delight, Tom realised that the jewel was cutting a magical gateway that would get them out of the catacombs.

Far above them, Tom could hear Malvel's castle groaning and crumbling. The collapsing catacombs must have damaged the very foundations of the castle.

"Stand close to me," Tom commanded, as more rocks fell around them.

His hand was still moving, the jewel drawing the last part of the new gateway. The darkness peeled away in a sharp, clear line. Beyond the freshly cut door, a purple mist swirled and beckoned.

"Tom," Elenna gasped, her eyes shining as she clasped Tom's hand. "Do you think this will take us back home to Avantia?"

"I hope so." Tom hardly dared to believe that they were just a step away from their beloved homeland.

In his mind he called to Arcta, telling the Good Beast to follow them through the gateway. Then he seized Storm's bridle, while Elenna grasped Silver's scruff, and together they dived into the cool purple mist.

The air stretched. Tom felt himself spinning. Bright lights glowed all around him.

"Goodbye, Tom and Elenna, goodbye..." Kerlo's voice echoed about them.

Tom started to say thank you to the gatekeeper, but an awful scream, full of fury, interrupted him. It was Malvel.

"You have not seen the last of me, Tom," Malvel screeched. "I will be victorious!"

But just as the words left Malvel's mouth, the wizard suddenly gave a shriek of fear. Tom could hear the sound of tumbling, crashing rock, and then nothing more.

Tom sensed the massive bulk of Arcta spinning beside him. Then the giant seemed to disappear, and Tom, Elenna, Storm and Silver landed on the familiar floor of King Hugo's throne room, where the king and Wizard Aduro were waiting expectantly for them.

"Welcome home." Aduro smiled, holding out his hands in greeting. "I knew you would prevail, Tom. Congratulations! You have defeated Malvel once again and, although I could not see as clearly as I would have liked, I believe that the Dark Wizard was crushed beneath the rubble of his own castle."

Tom felt a wave of relief surge through him as he embraced Aduro, but this was quickly replaced with panic. Where was Arcta? Had the giant somehow been pulled back into Gorgonia?

"Arcta has returned to his rightful place – in the mountains," said King Hugo, sensing his worry. He rose from his throne. "Well done, Tom. You are truly Avantia's greatest champion."

Tom bowed his head. While the King thanked Elenna for all her help, Tom looked out of one of the throne-room windows. The sky was sapphire-blue, and the sun shone gently down on the green land that surrounded the castle. Brightly coloured flags and pennants fluttered on the houses in the distance. They had escaped the swirling red fog of evil Gorgonia for ever.

"We are holding a feast in your

honour in the Great Hall today,"
King Hugo announced, as he
stroked Storm and Silver in turn.
"Avantia is impatient to welcome
home her heroes."

A liveried servant walked in
and draped a soft woollen blanket
over Storm's back, before leading
the stallion away for food and a
warm stable full of fresh bedding.
Tom looked down at the purple
jewel that still lay in his hand. He
slipped it into his belt. The row of
six jewels glowed fiercely, filling
the throne room with a rainbow of
light and power. The others looked
on in wonder.

Then King Hugo clapped an arm
around Tom's shoulder, and Aduro

walked between Elenna and Silver. Together, they all moved towards the palace stairway and down to the bustle of the Great Hall below, where the feast was being laid out. Brightly suited servants carried groaning trays of food, and musicians tuned their instruments in the minstrels' gallery. The citizens of Avantia were already streaming excitedly through the palace doors in their finest clothes, and the air was buzzing with chatter and laughter.

As Tom took his place at the top table between King Hugo and Elenna, his thoughts strayed to Malvel and Seth, the boy who had turned into a Beast. What had become of them? Had they really perished in the ruins of the castle? Then he thought of Odora and the Gorgonian rebels he had helped to escape into Avantia. Where were they now?

Shaking the thoughts from his head, he turned to Elenna and raised his glass. "Here's to the completion of another Beast Quest," Tom said. "I couldn't have done it without you, Elenna."

Elenna chinked her glass against Tom's and with her other hand fed some chicken to Silver, who sat at her feet. "You're welcome, Tom," she said cheerfully. Then she noticed her friend's serious expression. "But why don't you smile? Malvel has gone at last and it's all down to us!"

Tom drank deeply from his goblet, then grinned at his friend. He would allow himself to smile today – but only time would tell whether they had seen the last of Malvel!

CONGRATULATIONS, YOU HAVE COMPLETED THIS QUEST!

At the end of each chapter you were awarded a special gold coin. The QUEST in this book was worth an amazing 11 coins.

Look at the Beast Quest totem picture inside the back cover of this book to see how far you've come in your journey to become

MASTER OF THE BEASTS.

The more books you read, the more coins you will collect!

Do you want your own Beast Quest Totem?
1. Cut out and collect the coin below
2. Go to the Beast Quest website
3. Download and print out your totem
4. Add your coin to the totem
www.beastquest.co.uk/totem

Join Tom where this Beast Quest began in TORGOR THE MINOTAUR!

Read on for a sneak peek...

CHAPTER ONE

THROUGH THE LION'S GATE

The air tingled as Tom stepped into the lion's gate. It had appeared from the lake in Avantia after he had defeated Trillion, the evil three-headed lion, but Tom had no idea what lay on the other side.

His horse, Storm, reared up. "Steady, boy," Tom murmured, patting the stallion's glossy neck. Storm rolled his eyes nervously, but let Tom lead him forwards.

Tom's friend Elenna walked at his other side, with Silver close by. The grey wolf raised his muzzle and whined mournfully.

"We have to do this," Tom muttered through clenched teeth. "Malvel is here somewhere, I know it!"

"You're right, Tom." Elenna's voice was steady. "And we have to rescue Aduro."

Tom stepped out of the gate. A

flash of pure white light almost blinded him and a shudder of energy shot through his body. He stumbled and had to hold onto Storm's reins to keep himself from falling. He heard Elenna cry out in shock and Silver give a high-pitched howl.

When Tom's eyes cleared once more he found himself standing in a wasteland. Flat, featureless ground stretched out as far as he could see. A few plants with limp, dark leaves and sprawling stems poked up through the gritty soil, looking as if they were dead or dying. A gnarled tree, bare of leaves, stretched out its twisted branches towards the

four friends, and grey cloud hung
low beneath a red, swirling sky.
In the other direction lay desolate
marshes, with reed beds and scum-
filled pools. Huge bubbles rose to
the surface of the filthy water,
and burst with a gurgle and a
foul smell.

"Ugh!" Elenna choked out. "The
whole place reeks. Has Malvel
poisoned everything?"

Tom shivered and set his teeth
against the damp, cold air, while
Elenna pulled her shawl out of
Storm's saddlebag and drew it
tightly around her shoulders. "What
place is this?" she asked.

"It is the kingdom of Gorgonia,"
a stranger's voice said from behind

them.

They spun round to see a tall figure, dressed in ragged brown robes, standing just in front of the lion's gate. Tom reached for his sword. Silver let out a growl from deep inside his throat, and Elenna grasped her bow, taking an arrow from her quiver.

The newcomer leant on a staff of gnarled wood, staring at them. His head was bald. One eye was covered by an eye-patch, the other was a glittering grey.

"Who are you?" Tom asked boldly. He gripped his sword more tightly as the man shuffled forwards. "Don't come any closer."

The strange man's mouth twisted in amusement. "Have I threatened you?" He gave a bow. "My name is Kerlo. I am the gatekeeper of Gorgonia."

"Are you a servant to Malvel?"

Tom demanded.

"I am not," Kerlo said. "I do not serve any king or wizard. I simply watch the gate."

Tom wasn't sure he could trust this man, but there was no one else to ask for information. "What do you know about Malvel?" he said. "I have to find him. Does he live near here?"

Again Kerlo let out a short laugh. "Find Malvel? You and your friend should go back to Avantia before it is too late. Gorgonia does not welcome foolish heroes."

"We are no fools – we're here to rescue my friend, the wizard Aduro," Tom explained.

"And we're not going back

until we find him," Elenna added defiantly.

Kerlo smiled, showing two rows of blackened teeth. "Very well, if you insist..." He stretched out a hand, pointing across the marshland with a bony finger. "That is the best way forwards."

Then dark shadows began to swirl in front of the lion's gate, and the mysterious gatekeeper vanished into thin air.

Read
TORGOR THE MINOTAUR
to find out more!

FIGHT THE BEASTS,
FEAR THE MAGIC

Are you a BEAST QUEST mega fan?
Do you want to know about all the latest news,
competitions and books before anyone else?

Then join our Quest Club!

Visit the BEAST QUEST website
and sign up today!

www.beastquest.co.uk

Discover the new Beast Quest mobile game from

Available free on iOS and Android

Guide Tom on his Quest to free the Good Beasts
of Avantia from Malvel's evil spells.

Battle the Beasts, defeat the minions,
unearth the secrets and collect
rewards as you journey through the
Kingdom of Avantia.

DOWNLOAD THE APP TO BEGIN
THE ADVENTURE NOW!

Not final artwork. Produced and created by Miniclip SA and Beast Quest Ltd. All rights reserved.